Couture
Time Machine

Couture
Time Machine

By

CATHERINE STEWART

authorHOUSE®

AuthorHouse™
1663 Liberty Drive
Bloomington, IN 47403
www.authorhouse.com
Phone: 1-800-839-8640

Published by AuthorHouse 12/12/2014

ISBN: 978-1-4969-5887-7 (sc)
ISBN: 978-1-4969-5886-0 (e)

Library of Congress Control Number: 2014922212

Contents

Not that I am afraid, but there is very little time left.

~John Ashbery

Chapter One

Okay, I want to go on record and say that I know this story sounds crazy, but it really happened to me.

Let's start with me, which will set the stage. My name is Sukey well, not my real name…my nickname, but it stuck, what can you do? I'm thirty-ish and live in the Midwest, Michigan to be specific. I have a good job with a large company (you've heard of it, I'm just not going to name it) that has amazing benefits. I'm in leadership, but my job is not really exciting, know what I mean? I'm not curing any diseases or helping right some terrible wrong - just going through the motions Monday through Friday. I'm a brunette with shoulder length hair who is on the tall side, not really skinny, but not really fat either….well, a couple parts *are* fat but I cover those up. I have a passion for clothes. Not just clothes. Shoes, jewelry, purses, and watches; lately I'm into vintage. Prowling the re-sale shops in the area is like a treasure hunt, and then you don't look like everyone else. It is in a Detroit re-sale shop where my crazy story begins.

Chapter Two

It started out like any random Saturday in May. "Mary? It's Sukey, would you like to go vintage shopping with me today?". I called my good friend Mary in hopes that I did not have to go alone. Mary and I have been friends for years, since high school actually. She is not really into the fashion thing like I am. "I guess...I don't know why you would want to buy used clothes Suk, I just don't get it", she said. Mary is a little rough around the edges, that's why I like her so well; she will say whatever is on her mind, no filters at all. She and I are the same age, she is shorter than I am and has the cutest dish water blonde pixie haircut. "I told you I wash them or dry clean them after I buy them, some of the old stuff is so cool, the details and the tailoring are not to be believed", I hoped I had convinced her. "What's in it for me?" she asked. I coaxed her with her stomach, "I will buy you a fabulous lunch afterwards....deal?", she agreed and we planned for me to pick her up at her place in Eastpointe. Eastpointe is on the way to the store so it worked out perfectly. Eastpointe was re-named in the early 1990's; it used to be called East Detroit, but it was not East of Detroit. If you go East of Detroit you either end up in the Detroit River or Canada, which is one of the reasons it received its

3

CATHERINE STEWART

new moniker I imagine. The store we are headed to is on Woodward Avenue in Detroit. It is on the same exact site as the old J.L. Hudson's Department Store. The resale shop is so avant garde, you never know what you might find on any given day, they receive new (well, really old) shipments in all the time from across the country. Some of my most coveted pieces were found at Vintage Togs on Woodward.

I mentioned Hudson's for a couple of reasons. One reason is because it was a very nice department store that saw its start in Detroit. The other reason is my Mom used to work there. My Mom always dressed well. She would have on a completely fabulous look for day, head to toe, and go to the A & P for groceries (or Wrigley's or Great Scott). Hmmm, that might be where *I* get it. She died about six years ago. She and I would frequent Macy's (today's version of Hudson's) and spend the morning bargain hunting and end up eating lunch there where my Mom would always order the Maurice salad. She would have loved Vintage Togs on Woodward. I miss her still.

I arrive at Mary's about ten in the morning and honk the horn of my Granada Red 1964 Buick Riviera (What? I mentioned that I was from Michigan right?). Mary comes bouncing out the front door and rolls her eyes at my car. Mary is from Illinois and does not understand all of the charms of people from Michigan. Most people here do not have just one car, most people here only buy cars from the big three, and most people here have at least one old car. Also, most people here only buy from one car company, and for me it's General Motors. "Old car? Old clothes make sense then I guess" she says with a sarcastic smile on her cute little face. "Very funny" I say as I squeal the tires, and we're off. I tell her that Vintage Togs on Woodward is on the exact spot as the old Hudson's Department store. "Tell me why that's important", she says. No filters, remember. So I remind her that my Mom worked there for years, and it was THE store to shop at. At one time it was the tallest department store *in the world*, and it encompassed an entire city block with more than two million square feet. It was grand in scale, but also grand in its furnishings. The bank of brass tone elevators where you could see the all of the working parts would take your breath away as a kid, and there were white gloved elevator operators that ran them – such class. Unfortunately in 1998 it was demolished, which nearly broke my Mom's heart.

I was singing along with Bob Seger's *Roll Me Away* as we pulled into the parking lot. Vintage Togs on Woodward is a fairly large shop for a resale store. The minute you walk in the door there is a pleasant smell that reminds me of a library; old books. They also have this fantastic large old chandelier that hangs above the selling floor. "What exactly are you looking for?" Mary asks me. I respond with "Whatever speaks to me" which gets me another eye roll from Mary. I leave Mary to look at purses, or as my Mom called them pocketbooks and head straight to the couture section looking for buried treasure.

I am browsing through the dresses, and my hands encounter some of the most beautiful fabrics. I linger on more than one satin creation. Then I see it, and it's a size 8, hooray! It is a 1950's style dress for day. Looks like something one would wear to tea, I must have it. It is sea foam green, and, and, and now Mary is pulling on my arm. I look at her with contempt, "What?". She motions to this guy across the store and says, "See that cute guy, he is totally checkin' you out, hasn't taken his eyes offa you. Look… right now". I look at him, and sure enough *is* he cute, and he *is* looking at me. I'm never sure about men and what their intentions are. Yes, he is looking at me, but is he considering how much I look like his sister? Does he think I'm funny looking and have a big forehead or something? Or, is he truly interested in me and that is why he is looking? I go back to what piqued my interest, the green dress. "Mary, look at this dress, isn't it gorgeous?". She says, "That would look fab on you, you must try it on. Let's try and find some shoes and other stuff to go with it, so when you try it on you have a complete outfit." "What a great idea", I say and just like that I grab the dress and we are off to the shoes. By the way, that guy was bookish, really tall and cute – just my type.

Chapter Three

In the shoe area I am drawn to a pair of plain pumps with a rather pointed toe, they are cream colored and fabric, almost a bridesmaid dye-able type of shoe in size 7. The right shoe has a stain on the heel, probably from driving. No matter, I'm just trying them on for effect. One of the store employees approaches and asks, "Would you like me to start a fitting room for you?". "Yes, thanks" I reply. She tells me her name and that my selections will be in the last fitting room on the right. "You know what you need now?" Mary asks. "I have no earthly idea", I reply. "Other than that fine looking guy…..your outfit needs a hat, don't you think?". I say, "Yes to the hat, no to the guy". The hats are rather uninspired. There are some berets, but I associate those with the 60's or 70's. There are some with netting over the face, which is very cute, but not really my style. And then I see two that just might do the job. One is an oval shaped straw hat without a brim; it is a golden color with three small straw bows on the top, so chic. The other is looks like a flying saucer and is lavender, they would both look cute with the dress. Of course Mary has to put in her two cents. "Neither of them are green, the dress is green, your hat needs to match" she says. I remind her *yet again* that not all of the items that make up your look need to be in the same color family, it looks too matchy-matchy. Either of these two hats will go with the green dress. "Which one do you like more?" I ask her. She likes the golden straw number. I agree and head toward the fitting room handing my purse to Mary to hold for me. Over my shoulder I tell her "Stay right here, I will put this whole look together and come out to show you, be back in a jiff". She mumbles something about me showing *her* the look and showing *someone* else. I ignore her reference to the cute guy and head toward the last fitting room on the right. I did not know it at the time, of course, but that fitting room was about to change me…change my life…forever from that day forward (Wow that was a bold statement). I walked to the fitting room and turned the door knob as I entered.

Chapter Four

    The fitting room was quite pretty, it had flowered wall paper on the walls, five large brass hooks to hang my selections on, a generous three way mirror and two cute little chairs. The chairs looked vintage, like they belonged in front of a makeup table in a smart French ladies home from the 50's or 60's. They were both mauve moiré silk and were so cute, they were the kind of chair that had a skirt that went to the floor, very girly. The back of the chair was tufted with fabric buttons. I took a moment to look for a price tag. I then remembered why I was here and set about changing into the dress. This dress is so adorable; it has capped sleeves, a sea foam green underskirt, with an overskirt that is sheer cream chiffon with a delicate repeated flower design. It has a full 1950's skirt with darts on the bodice and a wide green satin sash. I step into the sweet dress and it fits like a dressmaker made it for me. I can't help but smile in the mirror. I imagine the chic woman who bought this dress wore it with a string of pearls, so cute. I am looking at myself in the three way mirror, turning left, turning right; the feel of the satin sash around my waist is so soft. Next the shoes, which don't seem exactly right with the dress, but they are the best option in the store. They fit, but are very pointy, not something that I would traditionally wear – I remind myself that this is just for fun. With the shoes on I stand a little straighter, shoulders back, this is definitely a feminine look. Should I show Mary now? Oh, right, the hat. I grab the hat and check it out on the underside. It has two combs that will help anchor it to my hair. I sit in one of the adorable chairs with a flourish, poised to put on the hat. I place the hat on my head, and what happens next is difficult to describe.

I find that I have fallen forward and I am now on my hands and knees. I feel as though I've had the wind knocked out of me, I literally cannot breathe. I'm blinking, my vision is not perfectly clear. What is going on? I take a gulp of air, and another, and find I am panting as if I've just run the fifty yard dash. My heart is racing. My vision clears and I look at my reflection in the mirror. I am quite pale. I close my eyes and take a couple more breaths. What the heck is going on? I sit back on my heels and look around. Things are not quite right. The fitting room door is now a red velvet curtain, how can that be? I close and open my eyes again. My heart is still racing. I hear voices. I hear a female employee in the fitting room talking to a customer. There was no one else in the fitting room area when *I* came in. The customer leaves. Now I hear one female employee talking to another. "Midge did you see who that was? That last customer was Mrs. Dodge. I just waited on Mrs. Dodge!". The other employee exclaimed, "Oh my stars". Their voices faded as they left the fitting room area. Who says "Oh my stars" anymore? That's odd. I crawl over to the curtain and peak out. I am the only person in the fitting room area. I am trying to process what exactly is going on. I hear bells or tones overhead – like what you would hear in an old time department store. I also smell a strong cotton smell, like brand new clothes. I see a sign through the parted curtain that says Woodward Shop. Oh my gosh! That can only mean one thing. How can this be? I am….I am in JL Hudson's Downtown Detroit Department Store.

Okay, get a grip Sukey girl. Maybe this is a dream. I should tell you that I have very vivid dreams in which I can recall colors and entire conversations the next morning. Sometimes I am even able to control the dreams. I am aware, while dreaming, that I am asleep and manipulate the dream to my liking – it's kind of fun. So perhaps this *is* a dream. I *think* I am in J L Hudson's somewhere in the 1950's. I traveled back in time. I traveled back in time? I need to re-group. I sit back down in one of the little chairs and think this through. Deep breath. I am going to walk out there and check it out, *that* is a certainty. My appearance is fine, nothing about me looks like current day, well not really. Except for my street clothes here in the fitting room. I fold them and tuck them under the skirt of one of the chairs along with my shoes and the plastic hangar. I peak out again and the coast is clear. I walk out with confidence and close the curtain behind me with the hope that no one else goes in there and discovers my belongings.

Sure enough I am in the Woodward Avenue Hudson's store sometime in the 1950's. How extraordinary. I walk out and see two very smartly dressed women talking about a dress. They are both dressed to the nines with gloves, high heels, matching handbags...the works. I don't have gloves, I hope that is not a dead giveaway that I don't belong. They are describing the dress as 'darling'. That is totally something my Mom would have said. Oh my gosh, my Mom! My Mom works here, I could walk around and find her. See my Mom while she is in her early 30's, talk with her even...my heart is racing again. I can't just stand here staring at people so I walk around as if I am shopping, trying to get a grip on myself and not start crying at the thought of seeing my Mom again – perhaps even conversing with her. I wander over near the men's department and there is a trio of sailors joking around. They are so handsome in their uniforms, with their hair slicked back. I overhear their conversation and they are discussing who is the better athlete; Al Kaline or Ted Lindsay. One sailor calls the other two "knuckleheads". I also smell their aftershave lotion, I think it's Old Spice? I keep walking, I don't want to draw attention to myself, but I want to take it all in. I see a lady with a baby in a stroller, or do they call them prams? That baby would now be older than me, how crazy is that? The

stroller is all metal tubing with a vinyl seat. The front bar
has colored wooden beads on it. I imagine this seat would
be so hot in the sun. A far cry from today's super strollers.
Now I am in the accessories department. I notice that my
hat and dress look appropriate, but my makeup is all wrong;
too muted compared with all of the other shoppers. Also, I
don't have gloves or a handbag, or should I say pocketbook?
Oh, big mistake, I don't have on any hosiery. That is a
huge faux pas in this time, I am probably looked upon as
homeless, or worse, a streetwalker! I am, however, enthralled
at the choice of items in the display cases. The cases are
real mahogany with gleaming glass on the front and top.
The stock of wallets is unique in that they are so small, and
everything is leather. I guess back then what did women
have in their wallets but some small bills and a driver's
license? That is something that I did not think of. Even
more surprising, there are more cigarette cases than wallets.
Some of the cigarette cases are rather fancy too. I suppose
you would need one with rhinestones for a black tie affair, it
would make a very smart cell phone case back in my time.
There are many sets of gloves to choose from as well, several
lengths, going all the way up the arm to the shoulder…
so refined. There is also an extensive selection of ladies
handkerchiefs and scarves. Prominent behind the counter
is a giant black cash register. It is then that a 'salesgirl'
approaches me and asks, "May I take anything out for you?".

I know it is hard to imagine, but everything is behind lock and key and you need a salesperson to show it to you, you cannot help yourself. She is very pretty and I notice her nametag says Vivian. Such an old fashioned name, but very high brow. I cautiously engage her in conversation about the gloves, careful to not ask anything that will give me away. The telephone behind the counter rings and she excuses herself to answer it, such gracious manners. I wander away so that she will forget about me. It is at this time when I notice I am drawing attention. Oh shoot, what do I do?

Leaning on one of the beautiful real wood pillars in the store is a gentleman in a suit. He is standing with his arms crossed and he is looking at me every thirty seconds or so. He is wearing a suit, but he is not really refined. He looks like a tough guy. I leave the accessories department and head to the handbags department which is quite busy, so I hope to blend in and escape the scrutiny of this guy. I am wandering around looking into the display cases, pausing every once in a while pretending interest. I look up and do not see the tough guy. I'm relieved. I complete my faux shopping of the handbags and spot him in a new location looking at me. Okay, what is going on? I stop and stare into the display case and try to think of why I am standing out. First of all I am very jumpy so that makes me suspicious, then there is my appearance, I do not look exactly like the rest of these women shopping here. I also am shopping without a purse of any kind, no wonder I look distrustful. Then, it dawns on me. He is a store detective. He thinks I am a thief, no - a shoplifter. I guess I don't blame him. I do not need this guy to take me to his office to question me with no identification on me. I have to shake this guy. I ask the salesgirl in the handbags department where the ladies room is. She points to her left and I see the sign hanging that she is referencing. I thank her and head off to the ladies room on a mission. The ladies room is right next to the dress department and the fitting room that transported me here. I go into the ladies room and notice there is a lady in a uniform who is a restroom attendant. I say good morning to her and go into a stall. Now what? It's not like I can hide out here for a long period of time, this lady will start to inquire whether or not I am feeling well. I take a few breaths and try to think of a way out of this predicament. I need to get back to the fitting room, that is for sure. I am not positive, but it feels like I have been gone from Mary, and my century, for about thirty minutes. She must be worried. Did she go into the fitting room and find me gone, or did she discover my clothes and think I was kidnapped?. I have to get back to her. One thing I know for sure, *I am* coming back here…to this time. I will be dressed correctly and *I will find my Mom*, maybe even talk with her. Just the thought of talking with her again gives me the courage I need to leave the ladies room. I exit the stall, wash my hands with powder soap (yuck) and dry them on a roll of fabric – remember those 'machines' that hung on the wall and you pulled the fabric down to get a clean length of fabric (yuck again)? I stand up straight, square my shoulders and exit the ladies room as if I belong in this store. I head for the Woodward Shop, where the fine dresses are and do not look around for the store detective. I do not even know if he is around observing me. I act as though I do not have a care in the world. I am browsing through the ladies dresses, taking my sweet time. I finally choose two and take them into the fitting room. I notice that once again I am the only person in here. Thank goodness! I round the corner, place the two dresses I picked out on a nearby rack and head for the fitting room that brought me here to this time. I cautiously approach. The curtain is still closed as I had left it. But does that mean someone is in there? I take a chance and brazenly peak in. No one is in there, thank goodness again! I go in and make sure I completely close the curtain behind me. I count to five and peek back out to make sure I made it without anyone noticing. Just then I see the back of the tough guy leaving the ladies fitting room. He followed me, and is now going for back up…or something. This is not good. I have to get back to my own time to escape. This guy is good. I look under the chair, and my belongings are still there. I sit back down and prepare myself for time travel knowing I will arrive back in my century out of breath and disoriented. As I raise my hands to remove my hat I hear a man's voice saying, "She went into the last fitting room on the right. Go in there and bring her out here".

Chapter Five

My next memory is of viewing myself in the mirror of the fitting room. As with the last time; I am short of breath. I notice that there is a fitting room door again and not a curtain, so I guess I am back in my own time. I am trying to focus and catch my breath. I am on my hands and knees again with the hat on the floor next to me. That is when I notice that my ears are ringing and I cannot hear anything going on around me so I do not know how long Mary was knocking on the fitting room door. She came in and was shocked to see me on the floor. I cannot imagine what was going through her mind in that moment. She looked panicked, I imagine that she called for help, but I am not certain as my hearing has not fully returned. She has my shoulders and is talking to me inches from my face; I'm not sure what she is saying. I only stare back at her with a blank look on my face. She helps me into one of the chairs and I guess she spoke with one of the employees of Vintage Togs on Woodward, because now there is a cup of water being offered to me. I take a few sips, a few deep breaths, and open and close my eyes a few times. My eyes begin to tear up, mostly from embarrassment. My hearing is returning because I hear the employee offer to call 911. I speak up then and say that I am okay (in a louder than normal voice), I just need to sit here for a few minutes. I plead with Mary using only my eyes; she gets the message and assures the employee we are okay. Mary closes the fitting room door so we are alone again. "What the hell? Did you faint?", she is asking two really good questions. What do I say to her? I have to convince her that I am okay. I tell her, "I am okay now, just need to catch my breath. How long have I been in the fitting room do you think?". This question really throws her, and now she is worried anew. She says, "I think maybe we should call 911 for you Sukey.....your freakin' me out". I try to assure her, "You trust me, right Mary? I need you to trust me now....I am fine and I will explain everything to you once we leave the store, I promise. Trust me?". She looks at me suspiciously, but agrees. I grab my belongings from under the chair and change back into my street clothes careful to hang the dress back on the hanger. Mary notices this and raises her eyebrows, "Why is your stuff under the chair?". "Trust Mary, trust" is all I say to her. I grab the dress, shoes and hat and head out of the fitting room. Mary hands me my purse – she had been holding it for me while I changed. We are back in the store now and people are looking at me. I imagine my face is red with the scrutiny. The cute tall guy is looking at me too, with concern. I try to look calm and collected as I head for the register to buy these items. "Why are you buying this stuff?" Mary is almost shouting at me.

She cannot understand my behavior of the last few minutes. This is totally out of character for me to be impetuous. I pay for my items and we exit the store as quickly as I can manage with my arm through Mary's to hurry her along. I hear the cute tall guy asking the store owner, as the door closes behind me, "Who is that woman that just purchased the green dress?".

Chapter Six

I manage to get Mary back into the Riviera, she is of course asking me questions all the way through the parking lot. We get in and I carefully place my dress in the back seat along with my hat and pumps. I crank my window down and turn down the radio. Why is it when you get back into the car the radio is always blaring, but when you parked the car the volume was just fine? I regretfully turn down Ted Nugent lamenting the fact that he has *Cat Scratch Fever* so that I can tackle the barrage of questions coming from Mary.

"Yes, I am fine". "Yes, I'm sure". "No, I do not need a doctor", "Don't be ridiculous I am not dying", "Yes, I am able to drive". "Please Mary, we have known each other for a long time. Trust me. I am fine. Now answer a question for me. How long was I in the fitting room? This is very important so answer me honestly." She says between five and ten minutes, she called out to me and I did not answer so she came near my fitting room door and called my name and when I did not answer a second time she came in and found me on the floor. Five or ten minutes? That *is* weird because I was gone at least thirty or forty minutes. I leave the parking lot and head north to the restaurant for lunch.

As I pass the store I notice the cute tall guy standing at the door, he has his hand raised in a wave. In an impulse I wave back. Why did I do that? I guess I am a completely different person now.

"That's it?" Mary is pretty mad. "That's all you're going to say?". "Yes, I do trust you, but I need more information than that....you faint in a fitting room, buy a dress and I am just supposed to shut up about it? Well, guess what? That's not going to happen. Your gonna start talking and start right now sister!". Wow she is *really* mad. How do I explain what I experienced without sounding like I'm psychotic? I convince her that I will tell her everything over lunch; I need to organize my thoughts.

"Where are we going anyway", she asks.

"To a restaurant in St. Clair Shores", I say.

"Why don't we take Lakeshore Drive?, It's such a pretty view".

"Oh really? The girl who is not from Michigan knows about Lakeshore Drive? Sure, we can go that route."

Lakeshore Drive is just that...it is a residential street with primarily glamorous homes on the West and Lake St. Clair to the East. It is a very pretty drive. I imagine the sunrise is stunning. We cruise along at low speed to check out the homes, picking out our favorites as I head up a side street that will take us to the restaurant. "You know Sukey, you looked really hot in that 1950's get up", says a still fuming Mary. I thank her, hot is not really what I was going for, but I appreciate the compliment all the same. "What is the deal with this restaurant anyway?" Mary inquires. I tell her that it is a great restaurant in St. Clair Shores; I go there all the time, it's on the lake. Hopefully we can sit in one of the booths by the window so I can tell my story to Mary with a small amount of privacy. When we arrive I motion to an empty booth, and get a go ahead nod from the hostess, and we sit by the window. I encourage Mary to order the Maurice salad. Which is julienne ham, turkey and swiss cheese on a bed of shredded iceberg lettuce with hardboiled egg. The real magic is in the creamy dressing. This was a salad that Hudson's was famous for, and my Mom loved, I think it is fitting that we both order this salad today (especially since *I* was just shopping at the Hudson's downtown store).

"Spill the beans", Mary says. "I am not sure where to start", I reply. She gives me a look and so I begin my story. Mary is a pretty free spirited person, she believes in karma and meditation so I hope with that kind of open mind that she can accept my story. I tell her that I am almost certain that it was when I donned the 1950's hat that I was transported to another time. My arrival to the 1950's was similar to my arrival back to our time. My eyes, ears and breathing was affected for both trips, but I consider it well worth it. It is at this time that I am gauging her reaction.

She is looking at me very seriously, with a slight frown on her face, her brow furrowed. I take that as a good sign and continue my story. I tell her about the store detective and how I believe he was on to me which is concerning, because I plan on going back. She stops me right there, "What do you mean? This time travel nonsense almost killed you, took the very breath from your body and you want to repeat this madness?", she is quite taken aback. I remind her that my Mom works there and if I have the opportunity to talk with my Mom one more time, even with her looking at me as a stranger, a customer, I am going to go through it again and Mary cannot stop me. Mary is staring at me blinking her eyes. She is quiet and I am not sure what is going through her brain. It is then that our salads are delivered, they look wonderful. I guess time travel makes one famished. We thank our waitress, and when I look back at Mary her eyes are welling up. She barely gets out these words in a whisper as she is so choked up, "You have to go back Sukey...you have to see your Mom again....I know what she meant to you and that you miss her. As a matter fact... I'm going with you. You need back up, and this sounds like such a cool adventure that I won't miss it. I'm going too". This is the last thing I expected her to say. My eyes fill with tears as well. I did not consider this. Will it still work with two people? How in the world did it work for me? "Mary are you sure?" I say "This is no picnic, I was really upset when

I arrived". Then she had a really good point that was hard to argue with, "Yeah, but you were alone and did not know what to expect, or even what was going on, now we both know and will be there for each other....I'm going and that's final". A big smile spread across my face. Mary's face lit up as well. "Let's do this", I say and Mary and I shake hands, time traveler partners. Oh boy!

Chapter Seven

It was about three days later when I called Mary from work to strategize. We have been calling each other every day since my voyage last Saturday at Vintage Togs on Woodward. Basically we have been brainstorming about how we are going to look when we travel back so that we do not look out of place as I certainly did on my first trip. Mary starts, "You know the square shape of your finger nails is all wrong, you have to go for a manicure and have them reshaped into an oval, you should probably have them painted fire engine red to match your new red lipstick. Back then your lip color and nail color just *had* to match." "Your right Mary, where did you get that little tidbit?" I ask. "The internet", she answered "there is all kinds of trivia related to the 1950's that will come in handy for us, I also e-mailed to you a list of slang words for that time. Like guess what Back Seat Bingo means?". "I have no earthly idea", I say. Mary is delighted to explain that it means necking in the back seat of a car. "You do understand we are not going back to the 1950's to make out with boys, these are boys mind you, that are now probably in their eighties?" I say. "I know, I know, I just thought that one was fun", she says. We talk about how our lip color has to be a strong bold color and our brows should be penciled strong also. Black cat-eye liner was also very hip. We talk about going for a consultation at a makeup counter and telling the staff that we are going to a 1950's party. We pencil this in for Saturday morning. "What about hairstyles", Mary asks. I tell her that I have been looking into it and her current style is right on target. "What does that mean", she asks me indignant. "Listen darling, you have a classic hairstyle and do not need to change a thing, it is a compliment", I say pleadingly. I remind her not to blow dry it too poufy as there were no true blow dryers back then. "What about your hair style", she asks. "I was looking at some photos online and saw one that might work, I am texting it to you right now", I say. It is a beautiful photo of Veronica Lake, now do not get me wrong…I do not look at all like Veronica, she was a gorgeous blonde, but I can get my hair into that style. I think I need to use Velcro rollers, or maybe a curling iron – they did have curling irons back then. They were not electrical; you heated it up on the stove believe it or not. "Wow Suk, very sultry and sexy", Mary says with a deep voice, she obviously got my text. "Mary, you know that is not me", I reply. "I don't know Suk, you have changed since last Saturday, I like this new you, you are more confident and self-assured". I agreed with her. I cannot explain it, but I do feel different, empowered even.

We hang up and agree to talk again when we get home. I give her homework, she has to find a 1950's outfit for herself somehow and we have to discuss when we will take this trip, and this *will* be a trip believe me.

Chapter Eight

It is now a few days later, Saturday mid-morning to be exact. We are just leaving the makeup store with our '1950's party makeup'. I think I can replicate this look on my own. Not sure about the cat-eye liner, it is a little racy for me, but we agree that together we can apply this makeup when the time comes. We take turns taking photos of each other so we have a record of what the makeup looks like in detail. Our plan is now to go to Mary's house in Eastpointe to try our 1950's hairstyles with the makeup and complete the look; I have brought my hat to see how it all works together for me. Mary also claims to have found a few dresses online that would work for the period, and she wants my opinion. We would need to buy it quick, because alternations might be needed and we are planning our 'trip' for two weeks from today.

Mary styles her hair first, and since it is short and effortless to begin with, she is done in a snap and with her 'new' makeup she looks like a living doll. Almost like an extra from the *I Love Lucy* show from the fifties. I am next and try a combination of curling iron with a medium barrel and Velcro rollers. I try to keep the curls with a generous supply of hairspray, and it holds for now. If there is any humidity that day it might fall. But, then I think, women have been fighting with humidity for years and years and I should not worry about it too much. With Mary's help curling the back we get pretty close to the Veronica Lake photo. Now I am about to add the hat when Mary practically tackles me to the ground knocking the hat out of my hand. "What in the world are you doing?", I ask with attitude. "You might go back in time right here in my bedroom", Mary says very seriously. I tell her that while I am not a time travel expert I think the travel is dependent on a magical mix of things: the old Hudson's site, the last fitting room, the period clothing – a complete outfit, and also a positive frame of mind. I am sure I was thinking of my Mom when I traveled the first time. I cautiously place the hat on my head, look at Mary, and nothing happened. "See, I have to be *there* in *that* fitting room in *that* store all dolled up for it to work", I report. "What makes you think I'm gonna to travel with you then?", she says. "I do not know for sure, I think we should hold hands though", is the best response I can come up with as I shrug my shoulders. Again, I am not a time travel expert.

I look pretty good with the hat, hair and makeup, and Mary agrees. "What about jewelry?", she asks. "I picture my look with pearls, sort of a 'ladies who lunch' look. I could wear my Mom's pearl necklace, but would that be weird? What if she is wearing the very same necklace that day?" I inquire. "I don't know Sukey, that might be hard to explain, do you think? It might also be good luck, or at the very least a conversation starter. Have you thought about that? What are you going to talk about? You can't say 'Hi Mom how is Grandma?' or anything like that", Mary is right. I have not figured out what to say yet, that requires a lot more reflection. If I go with pearls she could go with large beads, I saw that online, large bead necklaces with rhinestone earrings were everywhere and it looked so cute. "I have some necklaces and earring and bracelets at home that I know will work for your look", I say. Mary gives me a sarcastic look and says, "I just bet you do girl". She knows that I am a huge fan of accessories and have just about anything in just about any color. I also have two of my Mom's vintage watches. They are both very tiny with small faces. My Mom was a petite lady and so had very small wrists. I cannot wear either of these watches, but maybe Mary can. I make a mental note to find these watches and check them out.

"I need to tell you about my dream last night... my Mom was in it again, and I want your interpretation", I tell her with apprehension. "Oh, your dreams are always so good, do tell, and don't leave anything out", she says. I tell her that I am walking with purpose, not away from something but towards something. Soon I am jogging, and then running. I am now on a sidewalk in a residential area.

I realize then that it is the old neighborhood in Mount Clemens where I grew up. Everything looks just the same; everyone's grass is so green. I go to the side of the garage and go through the gate and into the backyard of our old home. I enter the house through the back door. All of this is noteworthy as I never entered the house this way, always through the garage or through the front door. I am in the kitchen now and my Mom is there. She is talking to me, but I do not respond, it is almost as if I cannot speak. She looks young, about the age of her engagement photo; her hair is just the same as that photo. She is wearing my new/old green dress, the one I just purchased from Vintage Togs on Woodward – the 1950's dress. In the background, no, in the shadows there is someone standing there, they are not making their presence obvious. I believe from the profile that it is my Dad. I do not recall anything from my Mom's conversation other than at the end she said, "Come back to me" (I'll tell you why that is significant in a minute). Then she looks to the figure in the shadows, who I believe to be my Dad, and she starts saying my Dad's name over and over and over, "Jack, Jack, Jack"….just kind of monotone and repetitive, almost annoyingly. It is at that time that I wake up with a start to a blackbird just outside my bedroom window calling, "Ack, ack, ack". "What do you think of that dream Mary?".

"Wow, that is a good one, I know exactly how to read that one".

"Oh really? Enlighten me".

"You are running towards your past, that part is easy, you go into the house in an unusual fashion 'cuz that is how you are traveling back in time".

"Amazing, you have it so far, continue".

"Your Mom looks young, 'cuz that is how she is going to look when we visit with her in two weeks. The part about her wearing your dress? I'm not sure about that; let's skip that part for now. I think the part about her talking and you listening is just that. She is speaking to you through your dreams and wants you to listen….she wants you to visit with her by going back in time. I think your Dad is in the shadows because he died so long ago. Now what does, 'Come back to me' mean?".

I explain to her, "There was a movie from around 1980 about time travel called *Somewhere in Time* that starred Christopher Reeve and Jane Seymour, did you ever see it?". Mary shakes her head no, and her eyes get big so I take that as a good sign and continue. "My Mom and I would watch this movie whenever it was on in re-runs. Most of it takes place on Mackinac Island, up north, at the Grand Hotel. In the movie the female lead, who is an old lady, tells the male lead, a man in his twenties to 'Come back to me' early on in the movie. It is a very important part of the movie you see because she wants him to travel back in time to resume their love affair in 1912. It is very romantic; you need to watch it sometime". Mary is still staring at me. "Are you all right Mary?", I ask. She exhales dramatically. "That is a sure sign from your Mom that she wants you travel back in time to her, don't you see?" she says raising her voice. While my dreams are vivid and quite amazing sometimes, I do not think too much about hidden meaning, or believe I need to alter my life because of my dreams – Mary obviously *does* put a lot of stock in dreams. I change the subject just then, to get her off of dreams. I am also unsettled by the green dress in my dream, I must admit.

Chapter Nine

"Okay lady, show me these dresses you are considering", I say to Mary as we are huddled around her laptop. The first dress is pink, has a full skirt, short sleeves that are cuffed, and a mandarin color with a vee neck. So very cute, it looks like a cotton sateen material with a slight sheen. Not hot pink, and not light pink, more of a rose tone. It will look so cute with Mary's dishwater blonde pixie hair. "Love, love, love", is all I say. She tells me to at least look at the second one. The second dress is navy blue, also has a full skirt, but is very different in every other way. It is sleeveless, has four pleats running the length of the skirt on the left side with an adorable bow at the waist. The bodice is rather plain, but the neckline is square and rather open. This dress would also look lovely on Mary, I like them both. I think the pink would be more flattering with her coloring, but let her decide.

I try to be non-committal as I say, "They are both period, so either one will work, which one do you feel you will look beautiful in?".

"I am leaning toward the pink getup, and it will make my waist look positively anorexic" she says. I roll my eyes and say, "Not that that is *the* goal, but you *are* right, it will look fabulous on you, you will simply glow in that shade of pink". She goes about the task of ordering it with express shipping to arrive well before our 'departure' date of a week from Saturday. "Now", she says, "to the hats, I have a few of those to show you too. This is so fun, okay, here is the first one". This hat is an abstract print in shades of light pink, rose pink and black on a field of ivory. If you squint your eyes the design looks like flowers, it is really an artsy piece. It is circular and has pleats on one side, and the fabric appears to be satin. This hat would look so adorable with the pink dress. I say, "Very cute, show me the other one to compare". The second hat is in a lavender color also circular – all hats of this period looked like flying saucers. Is this because of America's obsession with getting to the moon? This hat has a wider brim and looks like it might be crocheted. It would go with the dress, but the first hat I like a lot more. I try again to be diplomatic. "This one is cute too, which hat do you think would look better with your hairstyle?" I ask. She looks at me sideways, thinking, looks in the mirror at herself and nodding her head says definitively, "The pink!". I nod my head too with a big smile. She says, "Hooray, we're done". Mary has never really been a shopper, at least not in my book. I say, "Wait, what about shoes Darling?". She holds up one finger (not that one) to indicate one minute and runs off to her bedroom. She returns with some black leather pumps with a high skinny heel that have quite a pointed toe. "What do you think?" she says with a smile, I nod my head yes.

"Those will definitely work", I say "plus I think I have pocketbooks for both of us".

"What the heck is a pocketbook? Is this some other Michigan thing I don't know about?"

"No, a pocketbook is an old fashioned term for purse; we need to start using these words I think. I was also considering what would be in a pocketbook for a 1950's lady. I've come up with a comb, a fancy handkerchief, a compact, a lipstick, a very small set of keys with no key fob, and a wallet. I have also given thought to what to do about cash. I think we should go to a coin and stamp collector store and purchase some vintage money to have on us. I was thinking a fifty dollar bill from the forties would work." It was incorrect currency that did in Christopher Reeve in *Somewhere in Time* sending him back to his time before he was ready.

"Why the forties? We are going back to the fifties, right?" Mary inquires.

"Yes, we are going back to the fifties, but if you check your money right now you will have currency from five, ten or even twenty years ago, correct? Not all of your bills are from the last year, so I think if we each have a fifty dollar bill from the 1940's we should be all right", I counter.

I wait while she goes to get her purse (I mean pocketbook). She gets out her wallet and her eyebrows go up, "Hey, you're right, I just got three twenties from the ATM yesterday one is nine years old and the other two are five years old. I guess I never thought about it. What about smaller bills or coins from that decade? Don't we need those too?", she asks.

"Here is my theory, we are two young ladies out shopping, and maybe we just went to the bank and the teller gave us a fifty dollar bill to shop, sounds believable, right? Then if we do purchase something the Hudson's salesgirl —that's what they called them – will give us appropriately dated change…easy!" I finish with a grin.

"Sukey, you're good at this stuff. That is brilliant! Do you plan to buy something though?"

"Yes, I want a keepsake from this adventure and I intend to buy if from my Mom if my nerves hold out."

"Oh, me too, I want a keepsake and I want to talk to your Mom too, this is going to be so exciting, I can't wait!"

"One more thing, we have to talk about foundations".

"Foundations? What the heck are they?", Mary asks.

"That is what they referred to when referencing bras and girdles and such, because it is the foundation garments underneath that help to shape your clothing on the outside, make sense?"

"You want me to wear a girdle, are you serious girl?"

"I think we should, it will also make us stand up straight and walk like a lady. We need stockings and garter belts too, what do you say about that?"

Mary says with a mischievous grin, "Those I already have".

"Oh Mary, you are so bad", and now we are both giggling.

Chapter Ten

It is now Wednesday, ten days to go for our magical trip. I just got home from work and rush in the house to get out my check list to see what needs to be done before our adventure. I take off my work clothes, put on some yoga pants and a tank top, put my hair up in a high pony tail and sit on the couch with my list. Here is what we have so far, money, dresses, shoes, pocketbooks and hats. Ordered from the internet, to arrive by Saturday hopefully are bras, girdles, stockings and garter belts. Oh, and I ordered white cotton gloves for both of us too. I am so darn excited to play dress up, not to mention seeing my Mom one more time.

I have not been sleeping very well as of late. When I do sleep I have vivid dreams, mostly about me and my Mom. We are either shopping or having lunch out…which makes perfect sense as that describes our perfect Saturday together. Last night was no different. My dream started out with my Mom and I shopping in the shoe department of a large department store. I was seated; waiting for a sales person to bring out my size when from the back room comes a gentleman, dressed in a 1950's suit and tie with slicked back hair. He has about 5 shoe boxes stacked one on top of the other and his face is obscured by the shoe boxes. He is heading my way, as he approaches my chair he brings the boxes down and now I see his face. It is the tall cute guy (I *really* wish I knew his name) from Vintage Togs on Woodward. He settles in to help me fit the shoes and I am just staring at him with a slack jaw. My Mom is sitting next to me and while looking at her cute little watch says, "It's time to go now Sukey". That is when I wake up. I shake my head and remember that I am supposed to be checking my list. I make a few more notes then go into the kitchen to warm up some soup for dinner.

Chapter Eleven

"Did everything arrive in the shipment? Nothing was back ordered, right?" I ask Mary in a phone call on the Friday before our big adventure. "I have everything: bra, girdle, stockings and garter belt, it all fits too. The bra is very pointy, why did women put up with that?" she says. "I'm not sure, I think it was the style back then. You have everything you need, right?" I reply. She agrees that she is ready. We take the next few minutes to talk about prep before we leave for the store and our strategy once we get there. I will explain to the store employee that we are going to a 1950's party that night and need to try on our dresses (that we will have with us) with some other item from the store in the fitting room to complete the effect. That excuse should work. I will also bring with me some jewelry for Mary that will look great with her 50's dress. It is at this point in the conversation that I get quiet. I am thinking about my Mom again and what I am going to say to her, I am a bit nervous, I must admit.

"Sukey? Are you still there?"

"Yes, I was just thinking about talking with my Mom...what if I chicken out?"

"You know me, I'm never at a loss for words, I'll start a conversation and you'll jump in when you're ready. I've got your back girl."

"Thanks, I will need your support tomorrow that is for sure. I am so glad you decided to come with me. I'm going to need you."

"Are you kiddin' me, I can't wait, this is going to be a blast. Are you sure I can't bring my smartphone and snap a few photos?"

"No, we cannot bring anything with us from our time… that will surely cause trouble. We are just going to go back in time, shop around, have a conversation – perhaps buy something, then return, agree?"

"You say 'back in time' like it's no big deal", Mary says while laughing.

I'm laughing too when I say, "I know this whole thing is crazy, right?". We end the conversation with me telling Mary that I will be at her house at 11:30 am the next morning where we will be doing our hair and makeup.

I go to bed sure that I will not sleep a wink and say a little prayer that our adventure is everything we hope it will be. Adventure turns out to be an understatement.

Chapter Twelve

Today is the day we go back in time. Yikes! I pull into Mary's driveway with the radio blaring Motown music. It was Diana Ross and the Supremes singing "Stop in the name of Love", this is such a great song. I cut the engine and go about bringing all my gear into Mary's house. I have butterflies in my stomach. I feel like I'm going to the prom or something with all the prep around an outfit. I went to the prom in the early 80's and my dress was hideous, it was a purple polyester contraption that was quite disco. It is unusual to think that this green dress from the 50's is far more attractive. I let myself in Mary's front door and she comes into the front room to meet me with a giant smile from ear to ear. "Today's the day!" she says and gives me a big bear hug "Aren't you excited?" "Of course, I am....I am also very nervous". She gives me another hug and tells me this is going to be the biggest adventure of our lives. I go about the task of spreading everything out on Mary's davenport (look it up). I separate everything into a pile for me and a pile for her. We have our dresses in separate garment bags and then we have plain brown paper shopping backs for all of our accessories. I hand Mary her pocketbook and tell her to look inside. There is a small red leather wallet with a fifty dollar bill dated 1945, a handkerchief, a mirror and a comb within. My pocketbook has similar items inside. I tell her not to forget to put her lipstick into her bag when we are finished applying each other's makeup.

We go into her bathroom and set out all of our makeup. Mary begins applying my makeup for me and finishes it off with a dusting of powder to set it. I apply my own mascara and then start Mary's makeup for her. We both have a bold shade of red, but hers is a little softer as she is far more fair skinned than I am.

"What are you going to say to your Mom?" Mary asks.

"I'm not sure, I am just another customer, so the conversation would have to center around the merchandise I would think, what do you suggest?".

"Yes, start there, but you can always count on me to get you going girl".

"I know you and your ways, don't get carried away with that mouth now Darling. The last thing we need is you spouting off to a security guard and we end up in the Wayne County jail or something."

"Trust me, I can be very charming when I want to be. Are you done yet?"

"Yes, I'm done, you look so adorable. Put on a thick coat of mascara while I start on curling my hair."

I put our things into the car, Mary locks her front door and I start the car. Just then a car is driving by very slowly and a guy yells out, "Nice car!" I yell back, "Thanks". Mary rolls her eyes and asks, "Why are guys always commenting on this car?". "Jealous?" I say and back out. You would think that she would notice how guys always notice my Riv and she should get a cool car of her own. Just for fun, I squeal the tires.

We pull into the parking lot of Vintage Togs on Woodward. I roll up my window and sigh. Mary notices, "We have everything, stop worrying, this is going to be great" she says. We gather up all of our bags and head into the store. I notice a car pulling into the parking lot just then. The driver looks familiar, but I don't give it another thought. I have thoughts of my Mom on my mind and time travel… of all things.

Chapter Thirteen

A store employee comes right up to us, and she asks "May I help you? Do you have something to return?". Mary explains that we are going to a 50's party tonight and are looking for accessories to go with our antique outfits. Mary shows her our hip makeup and the employee falls for our ruse. She shows us to the fitting rooms and I make a point to go into the last one on the right saying that it is larger than the other two fitting rooms and we can share. We place our bags in the room and she shuts the door on our fantastical fitting room while we shop for phony accessories. We are looking at scarves when I hear a bell ring on the store entrance and another shopper enters. I don't pay much attention. I am just focused on getting a scarf and getting into the fitting room with the magical properties. Mary nudges my ribs with her elbow, and gestures with her chin to the store entrance. I look up and I swear it is like time slowed down, sort of like in an action movie or something. I know…I'm being dramatic or romantic or just plain dumb. But, listen, it was the tall cute guy from the last time I was in *this* store. I promise. He looked just as handsome as the last time. Now *I'm* staring. He looks over at me and Mary and gives us the most leg shaking smile, I almost fainted.

Okay, now I am exaggerating. But it was a great smile. Mary nudges me again and whisper-yells, "It's him!". I say, "I know, I know, I see. Please, let's concentrate and get into that fitting room before I lose my nerve". We both grab a scarf and head into our fitting room. I shut the door behind us, and lean on it with a sigh. "He's dreamy", Mary says and wags her eyebrows at me. I impolitely tell her to 'shut it' and go about changing into my dress. We both get into our dresses being careful to hide our current clothes under the two little skirted chairs in the room. Also, we take turns zipping each other up. Now we are both standing in front of the three way mirror and we are being careful not to put our hats on – I am confident that it is that movement that transports us back in time (but really, I have no idea). We look adorable, if I must say so myself. Hair and makeup are appropriate for the 50's, we have on our full skirt dresses with stocking and pumps. Accessories are right on point, complete with gloves and pocketbooks. Mary gives me a hug, she is very excited, I can tell.

"Okay, what do we do now, tap our heels together three times?" she asks sarcastically.

"No, you smart aleck, after all this fuss I hope it works. Let's sit down, the last thing we will do is put our hats on. Hold my hand, and have an open mind", I respond. We both sit down and I can see in the mirror we both have smiles on our faces, I grab Mary's hand. With our free hands we simultaneously put our hats on. My very next thought is, 'this wasn't so bad this time'. Now Mary on the other hand….

Chapter Fourteen

I notice once again that the fitting room door has changed into a curtain, so I know we were successful. Oh wait, where is Mary? I look down and she is lying on the floor as if she passed out. My head is a little foggy, but otherwise I am none the worse for wear. I immediately go to my knees at Mary's side and her eyes are rolled to the back of her head. I grab her shoulders and give a little shake calling her name, but not too loudly. I get no response, and immediately start to sweat. Remembering my First Aid and CPR training at work I check her pulse, and she has a pulse, thank God. I check her breathing, she is not breathing. She is *not* breathing! I shake her by the shoulders again calling her name, louder this time. I begin to panic – panic was not in my CPR training. If I begin giving her mouth to mouth and someone from the 50's comes into the fitting room what on earth are they going to think of us? It is at this time that Mary takes a large gulp of air and comes to. I take a deep breath as well, thank God she is okay. Her eyes flutter and she focuses on me. I have her hand now and I am telling her she is okay, and to just lay there and take a few breaths before she tries to sit up. She is breathing regularly, her eyes are huge and she is just looking at me blinking her eyes. She is not saying a word. Did I break her? Mary is never at a loss for words.

"Mary, you're okay Darling. You're okay." I say this with conviction, but is she okay? "Mary? Darling, please say something", I am pleading now. Trying to be quiet, but it is hard to be quiet when you're a little bit panicked. She rises up to her elbows, still blinking her eyes and finally says something, "Hot damn Sukey! Did we make it?" a big smile spreading across her cute little face. Whew! I take a cleansing breath and finally smile too. I help her to the chair, "Yes, Darling we have arrived, see how the fitting room door is a curtain now?" I am pointing to the curtain still trying to compose myself. She asks me what happened, why she was on the floor. I explain, to the best of my ability, what I experienced and how I found her lying on the floor not breathing.

"Okay, let's go", she says.

"Wait, let's get composed a minute, my legs are still shaking, and I want to re-apply my lipstick."

"Good idea", she says. She opens her pocketbook and I cannot believe my eyes. Mary has put her current day Michigan driver's license in her pocketbook to time travel.

"What are you doing with that?" I say a little too loudly. Oh no, what does this mean? What if someone sees this license? How on earth are we going to explain this?

"What? It's just my license, I don't go anywhere without it, it's just a habit, don't worry, nothing will happen, Sukey please don't have a meltdown, nothing will happen."

Then I say, "Damn it!", yes, the person who never swears said damn it. Mary's eyes nearly bugged out of her head, she knew then that I was <u>very</u> upset.

"Sukey, I'm sorry, you were not supposed to see it, nothing will happen. I would do nothing to sabotage this adventure. You know that. I want you to see your Mom so badly" her eyes start to water as she says this.

"I know, please don't cry, you will ruin your make up. Please, just keep it hidden." I respond and force out a smile. What was she thinking? We both re-apply our lipstick, then I peek out of the curtain and shockingly there are no employees in the fitting room and we got away with that whole conversation undetected. I wonder if women in the 1950's would go into one fitting room together like they do in my time? Oh well, I cannot stress about that now. We just have to walk out with an air of belonging and try to act natural. I ask her, "Ready? Remember everything we talked about? Don't talk too much, don't stare, act natural, act like you belong, act like a lady, stand up straight." I'm saying this like a drill sergeant.

"I'm ready" she says with a confident grin, her nose in the air ever so slightly.

"Let's shop" I say, and with that we both leave the fitting room, with a swish of our full skirts.

Chapter Fifteen

We are in the Woodward Shop, dress department of J. L. Hudson's Department Store. Mary has a bit of a wide eyed look about her as she is taking it all in. She is in control of herself, however. I walk over to a rack of dresses pretending to browse. Mary does the same. I tell her to look at the two ladies a few racks to our right. They are about our age, and are dressed so smartly. One of them is holding up to her chest a yellow cocktail dress saying, "What do you think Patsy? Is it me? Would it work for the DSO gala?". Mary looks at me and wags her eyebrows, "Oh my gosh" she says "We are really here, what is the DSO?". I knew this would happen. Mary is going to ask two hundred questions. "Darling, it stands for the Detroit Symphony Orchestra, of course" and I give her a little wink. She nods her head and we move on to another rack of dresses. I tell her to look around, nonchalantly, while I keep my head down pretending to browse so we don't look too conspicuous. "Tell me what you see", I say. Mary starts describing everything around her.

"Well first of all, I hear these strange bells. This must be what you were telling me about when you time traveled the first time. Some sort of communication with employees. It's kind of cool. I am also noticing that the racks and counters are all of high quality wood, and the floor is so clean and shiny it is positively gleaming. People are all dressed up, like they just came from church or something. Everyone is so put together; their outfits are all very chic. That is what you always say, right Suk? Chic?" I nod my head and tell her to go on; I can tell she is really enjoying herself. "The men are so hot, Sukey. They are all very well groomed; they all have short hair that has so much product in it… their hair looks greasy. But not in a gross way, in a ummm, polished way….yes, they look polished. Like their shoes. Very hot though. I see one, no, two ladies with hair just like mine, yea! This is so fun. I see this one guy in the next department and he is….oh, he just caught my eye. I am going to smile and look away, as if I am shy." I stop her right there, and grab her arm.

"Mary I need to look at me and only me right now, this is very important. We cannot draw any attention to ourselves. Not positive attention or negative attention. We are the color beige right now, remember? Do not, I repeat, do not look at that person again. Look at the floor. Walk on the other side of me so your back is to him to give him the message that you are not interested." She walks around to my right. "Okay, now look at me. Describe what the guy looked like to the best of your ability as I look over your shoulder to see if I can figure out which guy it was." She is looking at me like I am a little bit crazy until I remind her about the store detective from my last trip to J. L. Hudson.

"Do you see a guy with a bit of a five o'clock shadow who is wearing a suit and is hanging around not too far from the escalator?" I look around, and then I look back at Mary, and then I look back at the dress rack like I'm browsing. I do not see the man she is describing. I don't know if that is good or bad. I want to rule out this man as <u>not</u> being the store detective – seeing him is the *very last thing* we need. Well, besides Mary bringing with her current day Michigan driver's license, sheesh. I tell her to just keep looking at me for another minute while I browse, just to be sure.

I think we are safe, so we wander over to the accessories department pretending to shop. We see a very well dressed lady talking with her young daughter who looks to be about ten years old. The little girl is in a pink dress, tights and white Mary Janes. She is adorable. "Shirley" the Mother is saying to the little girl "be a lamb and go ask the escalator attendant 'do you happen to have the time' oh, and say please" the little girl scampered away. I say to the lady, "your daughter is darling". She thanks me with a big smile on her face, I notice that we have the same style of pearl earrings on and Mary and I walk on.

"Remind me", Mary asks "what department does your Mom work in?". That is a good question as she worked in a few different departments and I am not sure what year exactly that we have landed in. "I am not one hundred percent certain, but I think a good bet would be to start in the Women's and Misses Millinery Shop on the seventh floor", I say. Of course what followed was a diatribe on what millinery means. Now that we have *that* straight we decide to take the elevators as that is quite an experience in itself, and for Mary this is her first trip in a Hudson's elevator.

We go around the corner and there before us is a bank of ten to fifteen elevators, Mary audibly gasped. They are all glass and brass and are quite beautiful. Just then one opens with the ringing of a bell and the red arrow above lights up. We wait while a few stylishly dressed people file off, then we get on with a young couple. There is a gentleman running the elevator, he is wearing while gloves, a smile and very politely inquires "what floor please?". The young couple is going to the thirteenth floor – I think the restaurants are on that floor. I respond seven and he pushes some buttons and levers and the elevator gates close with a series of clanks. Mary is enthralled, I can tell, she does not know where to look as there is so much elegance around her. There is a gorgeous light fixture overhead, and this is *just* the elevator. We arrive on seven and with a few more lever pulls and little more clanking the doors open and we thank the gentleman elevator operator and step off. I might be just minutes from seeing my Mom and actually talking with her. I grab Mary's hand as we walk towards the Women's Neckwear department. As we walk on we pass other elevators that are whizzing by, out of the corner of my eye I think I see the store detective on a passing car, but dismiss the thought instantly as nerves.

Chapter Sixteen

Mary and I are browsing at ladies scarves and I notice that just to our right is the millinery department. Mary follows my line of sight and asks, "What if she isn't working today, have you even thought of that possibility? Don't worry though, I'm still having a blast and I'm glad that we came. Maybe we can come back. Are you okay?". She noticed I am staring and not talking nor listening to her prattle on.

"She's right there" I manage to squeak out.

"What? Where? Which lady is she?"

"Give me a minute, all right? She is the lady in the blue suit", I whisper. I cannot stop staring at her. She looks so young. Her hair is dark brown, short and curly/wavy. She has on a form fitting blue suit that looks like it might be raw silk. The sleeves are three quarter length with white cuffs and the collar also is white. At the throat she has a pink silk rose pinned on. That is *so* her, she loved pins. That is all that I can see as she is behind the counter talking to a customer. "Mary? Do you see her?" I am looking around, now Mary is gone. Where in the world did she go? Heavens to Betsy! She is heading over to my Mom and motioning me to follow. My feet will not move for a minute. I am still staring at my Mom

I cannot believe she is right there. The next thing I know there is a person standing at my side, my peripheral vision picks up someone to my left. Oh no, it is the store detective. The very same man from my first visit back in time. He has the same cheap suit on and five o'clock shadow. He flashes a very impressive and intimidating badge at me. "My name is Elmer Johnson and I am a lieutenant in the loss prevention department at J. L. Hudson's….I have been observing you and have a few questions" he says this with a very satisfied smirk on his face. I am so frightened, I say nothing, my jaw is slack I probably look like someone with a feeble mind. "Well?" he says rather indignant, "cat got your tongue?". The following is all that I say, "I, I, I ccccan't". Then Mary shows up and grabs my elbow. Oh great, what on earth is she going to say. We are going to 1950's jail or something for sure. Then Mary confronts the guy and she is unbelievable, I wish I had an academy award in my pocketbook for the girl.

Chapter Seventeen

"I beg your pardon" Mary says raising her voice, her hand firmly holding my elbow as if I am a child. "Is there a problem here?" she is completely ignoring me and speaking to the store detective.

"Yes, there *is* a problem as a matter of fact. I am Elmer Johnson and I am a lieutenant in the loss prevention department at J. L. Hudson's (he flashes his badge at Mary). I have been observing this woman here (gesturing toward me) for some time and her behavior is very abnormal. I intend to take her to the loss prevention department on the nineteenth floor for questioning and to look in that handbag for stolen goods."

Mary says with venom in her voice, "Let me see that badge?". For some reason he listens to her and shows it to her. She appears to study it and then hands it back to him. All this time I am just standing there like a dolt looking back and forth between Mary and the store detective.

Then the show starts, "My name is Dr. Joyce Brothers" this is Mary speaking might I remind you, "and this is my ward (gesturing to me) Miss Gertrude Olds. Does that name mean anything to you sir?" she is just dripping with sarcasm at this point and her voice is getting louder.

"Perhaps you have heard of the Oldsmobile? Gertrude Olds is a direct descendent and heir of Ransom Olds the creator and inventor of the Oldsmobile motor car. She is of frail condition and this outing to your store is a part of her recovery. Now look here! She is bothering no one, certainly has not stolen anything from this establishment. If you persist in this folly I will be forced to press charges on behalf of the Olds estate. Do we have an understanding my good sir?". I am still just standing there staring, I might even be drooling, but that would help Mary's elaborate story wouldn't it?

"My deepest apologizes Madam" says the detective with a slight bow to me and a slight bow to Dr. Joyce. He is now looking at me with pity and a little revulsion. He says, "I was gravely mistaken and I shall take my leave now" and walks away at a quick pace.

Once he rounds the corner near the elevators I exhale and hit Mary playfully in the arm. She is giggling. "You are something else! An evil genius I suppose. When did you learn about Ransom Olds, are you holding out on me?" I am flabbergasted. She bats her eyes at me, "You just never know what I am going to say do you Sukey girl?". Mary just got us out of a jam with that fellow. He was pretty serious about his job, and I am not sure what would have happened to us if he had persisted in his claim and taken us to the nineteenth floor to his offices. Whew, dodged a bullet there.

I am <u>very glad</u> that Mary has come along now. I give her a big hug and all of my anxiety of this trip is gone. Now I just have to 'meet' my Mom. She grabs my hand and says with a grin, "Come on, let's go meet the stylish 50's lady in the hat department…I mean millinery department", and we walk off together with renewed vigor.

Chapter Eighteen

We approach a counter of hats and notice that the more elaborate hats are in the case and begin to look around. My Mom is talking with a gorgeous lady, she could be a model she is so stunning. The model is wearing a very form fitting off white dress with a large patent leather belt and matching pumps. The hat she is trying on is very fancy and looks like something one would wear in Paris. It is tilted to the right on her head with a small amount of beading and feathers that curve down to her neck. She looks striking. My Mom makes the sale and they go about completing the transaction. My Mom produces a very expensive looking hunter green box from beneath the counter. Inside is a nest of cream colored tissue paper. My Mom wraps the hat very carefully and places it in the box. The box is then fastened with a beautiful ribbon. If not for the Hudson's logo it would look like it was gift wrapped. Mary and I move in a little closer to hear their conversation. My Mom places the box into a shopping bag and staples it closed with the receipt prominent on the front and says, "Thank you so much Miss Fisher your purchase will arrive at your home on Rose Terrace in Grosse Pointe by Wednesday of next week. Here is your copy of the receipt. Have a good weekend!". Oh my goodness, my Mom's voice, my heart is pounding. "Thank you ever so much for your help today Trixie, you know you're my favorite salesgirl, bye bye". Yes, I know, I know, another unfortunate nickname. My Mom's given name is Theodora; it is some sort of family name on her Father's side of the family. When she was very little someone gave her the nickname and she has been Trixie ever since. The name fits her though. As the model saunters off my Mom turns her attention to Mary and I. I think…'here we go', and just then I notice three ladies walk up with their arms linked. They are Hudson's employees, I can tell by their name tags. They have the coolest names, Maxine, Sally and Ginny. Maxine is the leader of this group, you can just tell. She has died her hair cherry red and has lips to match, she is *no* wall flower. Maxine says to my Mom, "How's tricks?" all four women crack up. Apparently this is their little joke. My Mom turns to them and says, "Just a minute girls" holding up one finger. To Mary and I she says, "Sorry about my rowdy girl friends…how may I help you?". Mary pipes up and says "We are just browsing and can't decide. If you are going on your break with your gal pals please go ahead, we will still be here when you get back, have fun!". Mary is a genius, have I said that already? My Mom says, "Oh, that is so sweet of you girls, thank you, I will be back in a flash, look around to your heart's content". They walk off together arm in arm; you can tell they are work buddies. I hear my Mom say to

Maxine, "The girl in green looks like Jack's sister, Clara". My Mom thinks I look like my Aunt Clara, of course I've always been told I look like my Dad, and my Mom thinks I look familiar. That is so bizarre.

Mary and I have a few minutes alone. "Where did you come up with that Dr. Joyce Brothers story?" I ask "because it was brilliant". Mary reminds me that in high school she took a drama class and was in a few plays. "Obviously that is the store detective that was following me on my last visit, I am glad he is gone for now. But I think we need to keep our eyes open to him returning, or perhaps another person watching us, because we definitely are exhibiting unusual behavior" I say. Mary nods her head in agreement and takes an extra look around the store.

She says, "What is our strategy when your Mom returns?".

I reply, "I'm not sure, but what I *do* know is that we cannot try on any hats".

"What? Why? How are we going to buy something from your Mom then? I thought that was the whole idea."

"Yes, I intend to make a purchase. But keep in mind my theory that it is our hats that are the key to our time travel. If we remove them I am not sure what will happen. I don't want to take the chance. So, our hats must stay on. Agreed?

"Agreed, but how do we shop for and purchase a hat without trying one on?"

"Tell me what you think of this....I cannot try on a hat as the hat I have *on* is very secure with combs and pins and removing it will muss up my hair. I can also at that time ask her about the return policy to keep the conversation going."

"Good one Sukey that is a believable story". We continue to browse until we see the motley crew of my Mom and her three friends return from their break. They are laughing walking arm in arm and are so darn cute.

Chapter Nineteen

Maxine, the ring leader, is speaking "Okay, so we are all in agreement? 7:30 tonight at the Belle Isle fountain. I will tell Harry that we will meet him and his pals at the Casino at 7:45. Don't chicken out on us Trix, got it? See you later alligator" and the three gals sashay off with a sway of their hips. By the way Harry is my Mom's brother's name.

My Mom turns to us, "Thank you so much for waiting for me, don't pay any mind to my friends, they really are nice girls. Now, what can I show you?"

Of course Mary pipes up, "My friend here is looking for a special hat for an upcoming wedding…aren't you Sukey?"

I stammer while looking at my young Mother (who died six years ago), "Why….yes, yes I am. I am looking for a special hat", I sound like a parrot. I catch Mary's eye and she is giving me a look that reads 'get yourself together'. My Mom is looking at the shelves behind her and into the display cases. She turns to me, looking me in the eye. She is asking me something, but I am just staring back at her taking in her face and features, trying to commit this moment to memory. She is looking at me questioningly now. I exhale when I realize I was holding my breath. I say, "I beg your pardon?", and my Mom says, "What is the color of the dress you will be wearing?". I manage a smile now, and she smiles back. I take another breath and say "Black and white".

"You look so familiar to me, did you go to Pershing High?", my Mom is asking me if I went to her high school. Think fast…my high school did not exist in the 1950's.

"No, I went to Mount Clemens High" I say (sorry L'Anse Creuse North Crusaders for the betrayal). "I guess I have a common face".

"What do you think of hats with a veil? This style is in vogue now," my Mom is back to business, whew.

"I don't think a veil is for me, what do you have that is brand new?" I ask. She looks around the other side of the counter.

Mary whispers to me, "Good save on the high school question, you're doing great, keep it up. I'm here for you if you get stuck." I love that girl.

My Mom comes back with two options. The first one is entirely black and it is shaped sort of like a bucket. It looks like something Mamie Eisenhower would wear. I shake my head no at that one. The second one is very pretty. It is a black hat with a large brim and a wide white satin ribbon that trails down the brim in the back. It is beautiful. I can't help but think I have seen it before. I take the hat from her and it dawns on me that Audrey Hepburn wears this hat in *Breakfast at Tiffany's*. Maybe this movie hasn't come out yet. It is perfect, I love it.

"This hat would look lovely with your big brown eyes", my Mom says, "Why don't you try it on?".

"Oh, I can't....my hair would be a fright if I took my hat off now." Turning to Mary I ask her, holding the hat over my head in hover mode, "What do you think Mary.... is it me?".

Mary wags her eyebrows at me, "It is divine. You must get it, how much is it?".

My Mom looks at the Hudson's tag and looks disappointed, "It's pretty expensive, I'm sorry, I should have asked you what price point to be respectful of. It is seventy-five dollars." Obviously in this decade that is an extreme amount of money to pay for a hat.

"I can afford that, right Mary? You can loan me some money......um, until I get paid next week, right?" that would still leave Mary with about twenty-five dollars to buy her souvenir.

"Yes! You must buy this hat, it's meant to be" replies Mary who is just beaming.

"Great, thank you" I say to Mary. I turn to my Mom and say with confidence, "I'll take it".

My Mom nods her head and goes over to the cash register. Turning to me she says, "Cash or Hudson's charge?" I say, "Cash please". My Mom turns her back to us as she packages up my new hat in the fancy box with the dark green satin ribbon. I open my pocket book and get out my fifty dollar bill. Mary opens hers to get out *her* fifty dollar bill and we both spot her Michigan Driver's License. She quickly closes her bag while I roll my eyes at her. She squeezes her hand into her pocketbook and draws out the fifty dollar bill with a sigh, and hands it to me. Just then my Mom turns back around and asks if I would like my new hat delivered to my home free of charge. I reply, "Oh, no thank you I want to put it on tonight when I get home with my dress. I can't wait to see both pieces on together. Do you think I should wear my hair up or down with the hat?". Both ladies say I should wear it up and I agree.

Then my Mom asks me a question I was not prepared for and I almost dropped the ball. She asks me my name, for the receipt. Back then handwritten receipts were used with carbon paper. Oh no, what do I say? Mary is looking at me with apprehension.

"Sukey is my nickname, you don't want that on the receipt", I say stalling. "My full name is….Sandra Bullock" I say with conviction. Mary is looking at me like she is about to burst out laughing. I look back at her as if to say 'be good'. My Mom completes the transaction and hands me my hat box and receipt. "If you have the time Miss Bullock", she says "try to get up to the thirteenth floor to the Georgian Room Restaurant they have a great salad up there that you simply must try it is called the Maurice salad and I highly recommend it".

"Maybe we will" I say with a big smile on my face knowing that that is her most favorite salad in the world. I know now that my encounter with my Mom is coming to an end, which is sad.

"Thank you so much for shopping at J. L. Hudson Miss Bullock, please come again", she says. I thank her and Mary thanks her. We begin to walk away. My Mom then starts waiting on another customer, a woman with a little girl that looks to be about five years old. My Mom greets the woman and says to the little girl, "Hello lady, how are you?". We round the corner into the next department and I start to tear up. Lady is what my Mom used to call me when I was little….when I was big too. I can't believe I was just talking with my Mom, how extraordinary. Mary squeezes my arm and tells me how great I did. We head back to the elevators to go down to the main floor. Waiting at the bank of elevators is a small group of shoppers. There is a very handsome man in a navy blue suit who gives Mary the once over. He says hello to her, she says hello back in her sexy-girl voice. Oh no, don't fall apart on me now Mary.

Chapter Twenty

We enter the down elevator car and so does the navy blue suit. Mary is standing next to him and is flashing her best 'I'm single' smile. I know this because I have seen it on several occasions. Mary is the type of girl that attracts all kinds of men, from 18 years old to 88 years old. Men love Mary, and what's not to love? She is a spunky little blonde with a cute smile, flirty personality and she knows the effect she has on men – this can be a lethal combination. I take half a step closer to Mary. The navy blue suit is about to make his move, I can *just* tell. "Were you at the Fox Theatre last night?", he asks her. Without missing a beat she says, "Maybe, who wants to know?". Oh great, here we go. It is at this moment I notice the gold ring on the navy blue suit's left hand. "I'm the stage manager at the Fox and thought I saw you in the chorus" he says. The elevator doors open to the main floor and the three of us step off. I put my arm through Mary's and bring this little production to a close with the following remark, "I think I know your wife…. what is her first name? Is it Esther?". He becomes flustered then, poor guy. He stammers, "Um no, my wife's name is Florence, have a nice afternoon ladies" he tipped his hat at us and scurried off towards the Farmer Street exit. Mary turned to me frowning, "Hey, that wasn't very nice Sukey". I give her a smirk that says 'I know you Darling' and we move on towards the women's accessories. As we are walking I swear I see Mr. Store Detective again. I cannot confirm this, and do not share my suspicions with Mary, but I am looking around more often now, I am so jumpy. Mary is looking at the women's gloves. I know that she wants a souvenir from this trip and I am going to help her get some kind of memento to remember the day. Mary is talking with the sales girl about leather gloves. I take a moment to look at the receipt for my hat. I recognize my Mom's handwriting right away. Very pretty cursive handwriting and notice the date, June 6, 1953. Now I know what the year is…how fascinating. Mary chose a pair of leather gloves in a burgundy color. They are very fine leather and cost about $20 so she is all set. She gives the sales girl her real name, and I think why not because Mary's family is from Illinois and she has not been born yet. So what is the harm? They conclude their transaction and we head back to the Woodward Shop which is the fine dress department with the magical fitting room.

Chapter Twenty One

We browse around the dress department until a few shoppers lose interest in dresses and move on to another department. It appears as though we are the only people in the dress department and it also appears as though there is no one in the fitting room, perfect timing. We start towards the fitting room to make our exit from 1953 when I see the Hudson's store detective, Elmer Johnson walking towards us with purpose. I grab Mary's arm and pick up the pace. I hear him several steps behind us saying "Excuse me a minute, I need to talk to you two". I say to Mary, "We have got to go". We round the fitting room entrance just in time. Mary is fumbling with her pocketbook; she is trying to put her new gloves into her bag for easier travel. I know this guy cannot go into the ladies fitting room, it just would not be proper. We make it to 'our fitting room' safely. I close the curtain and Mary and I sit down in the two little chairs. We both have our pocketbooks on our arms. I have my hat purchase on my lap. We look at each other in the three way mirror. "Ready? I ask her. "I'm ready" she says. As we clasp hands we both move simultaneously to remove our hats, and we are transported back in time once again. Our 1953 trip was completely successful, or so I believed.

Chapter Twenty Two

Similar to my previous trip I have landed on my hands and knees and my hearing seems to be impaired. My pocketbook is still on my arm and my newly purchased hat made it back too, it is on the floor next to me. I shake my head a few times to work out the cobwebs associated with time travel. I notice Mary on the floor next to me. Somehow she is on her back, staring up at the ceiling. Her pocketbook is on her arm, however the clasp has come open and her new gloves are in her lap. I grab her upper arm and begin shaking it saying her name over and over. I am probably saying it too loud, but as my hearing has not returned yet there is not much I can do about that. Mary begins to blink in an exaggerated fashion. Good, she is coming back to me. I keep my hand on her arm and I am reassuring her that she is all right, but I am probably shouting at her. Oh well. I try to adjust my volume to what I hope is a normal tone or a whisper. Just then the fitting room door opens and it is one of the ladies that work at Vintage Togs on Woodward. I'm sure we are making a commotion and she is checking to see if we are all right. She is concerned to see us both on the floor. I manage a smile, I hope I am not shouting and tell her we are all right. "We just fell off of our high heels, ha ha" I

87

say as I roll my eyes at her. She smiles as she closes the door and says we look cute in our costumes. She probably thinks we are two complete air heads. Mary is sitting up now and she turns to me and asks, "Are we okay? Are we back to normal?". Oh good, my hearing has almost completely returned. I respond, "We are okay, but far from normal" as I grin at her "Do you feel all right?". She nods her head yes and I help her into the fitting room chair. She notices her purse is unclasped, "Oh no, where are my new gloves?" she asks. I point to the floor where they have fallen.

She gets a sparkle in her eye as she turns to me and gives me a great big hug, "We made it Sukey girl. We traveled back in time and saw your Mom. What do you say, huh?".

"It was pretty great, wasn't it? Thank you a million times for coming with me, I don't think I could have done it without you. Love you" I say getting choked up.

"Love you too. What are we gonna do now to top this adventure?".

I say, "I'm good for a while I think, let's get changed".

We change back into our current day clothes, pack up our outfits and come out of the fitting rooms with the two scarves that we took in there to try on with our ensembles. Mary walks over to put the scarves back on the shelf, but I change my mind....I think I will buy this scarf as a further souvenir of our tremendous day. I hand all of my packages over to Mary and head to the checkout to buy my scarf. I hear one of the employees ask Mary where she got the old Hudson's package. I give her a look that says 'you are on your own'. I know Mary can handle these questions, Mary can handle anything, and she's terrific. When I get to the checkout I hear someone just behind me say, "Well, hello again". I turn around and see that it is the cute tall guy. That's right…he was in the store when we entered the fitting room…..it seems like so long ago. It probably was only fifteen minutes to him. My face lights up when I see him, I can't help it he is just *so* cute. I manage to say hello, and he extends his hand to shake mine. "My name is John and…..and I think we have met before". Tall, cute and a little shy, I'm a goner I think as I shake his hand. "My name is Sukey, nice to meet you John", I manage to say. Mary has impeccable timing as she shows up at my side and says, "Look at you two holding hands, hi I'm Mary and this is Sukey, she *is* single ya know?". Wasn't I just saying how I could not live without her? Oh boy. I hand my credit card to the employee ringing up my scarf then turn back to him, "Please excuse my friend, she does not leave the house very often", I say to cute tall shy guy named John. He is grinning at the both of us and says, "Sukey? What kind of name is that?". The guy ringing up my scarf is saying, "Catherine?

Catherine? Catherine, I need your signature right here please". I turn to sign for my scarf. John is looking at me and says, "I like Catherine a whole lot better than Sukey…. will you two ladies accompany me to lunch?".

Epilogue

A most curious case has arisen today. Two female suspects presented on the main floor this noon. I proceeded to follow at a distance. Both women appeared to be well dressed, one a blonde and one a brunette, however their behavior was abnormal. I say abnormal as they both appeared to be frenzied. The brunette suspect was prone to crying jags and looking about the store in a hysterical fashion. The blonde female was definitely in charge. I ghosted them up to the seventh floor certain that confronting them would elicit a confession of some sort. I was bluffing however as I did not observe them lift any merchandise. When I spoke with them the blonde female took control of the conversation and gave me some convoluted story about being the caretaker for the brunette who was an Oldsmobile heiress. I was so taken aback by the believable story that I apologized and took my leave to follow up. I returned to the security office and consulted with one of my colleagues, Mr. Sherman Cooper [Security Corporal Second Class], who informed me, with no hesitation, that there were no Oldsmobile female heirs. At this juncture I continued my pursuit of the two female suspects albeit at a distance. I tracked their whereabouts to the Women's Millinery department where a purchase was made and I procured a copy of the receipt. The brunette suspect's name is Sandra Bullock, I am certain I have viewed her in the store on one other occasion in which she was also acting strangely. The blonde suspect also made a purchase, in the Women's glove department, and gave her name as Mary Ostrowski. What happens next is most curious. Both women proceed to the Women's dress department where I continued pursuit and observation at a distance. I felt I had them at a disadvantage, and had them cornered as they were heading into the Women's fitting room, where there was no egress. I called out to them and knowing that I now knew their ruse they rushed into the fitting room seeking asylum. The blonde suspect, however, gave away her hand as she dropped a key piece of evidence in her haste. Strangely, both women entered the same fitting room and inexplicitly disappeared after that. I quickly got the attention of a sales girl on the floor who went into the fitting room and came out telling me it was empty. I looked for myself and it was indeed empty. I do not know where they went. The blonde suspect left behind some form of identification card. It was most unusual. It had markings that indicated it was a piece of Michigan identification. The city it had listed was Eastpointe Michigan, and after confirmation there is no Eastpointe Michigan. It listed the woman's name as Mary Margaret Ostrowski. The bizarre fact was that this piece of identification was due to expire in December in the year of our Lord 2017, which is some sixty-four years from now. The evidence was tagged [J. L. Hudson evidence tag 529] and turned over to the Michigan state police on 12 June 1953. END OF REPORT.

Lieutenant Elmer Johnson
Lieutenant Elmer Johnson

CC: Michigan State Police, Trooper Samuel G. Thompson

Couture Time Machine is fictional and exists only in the realm of the imagination. The J. L. Hudson's Department Store was real, of course, I am thankful *to Images of America Hudson's Detroit's Legendary Department Store*, by Michael Hauser and Marianne Weldon a book which I used as a reference.